45 p

The Young World Library is a series designed for the young reader. The stories are taken from some of the world's best-known novels, plays, legends, operas and ballets. They have been simplified and re-told in a way which keeps close to the spirit of the original, while bringing everything within the immediate grasp of the young reader's understanding of words. Equally important are the illustrations, which have been chosen both to delight the eye and to match the special character of each story. Thus the Young World Library offers young readers a unique stepping stone towards the use and enjoyment of books. It also introduces them in a lively, up-to-date way to many famous stories and characters from the wonderful world of literature and the performing arts.

Series Editor: Alan Blackwood

© 1974 Thomas Nelson & Sons Limited.
SBN 72381027 3
Printed in Great Britain by A. Wheaton & Co., Exeter.

PETRUSHKA THE PUPPET

Adapted and told by
Alan Blackwood

Illustrated by
Belinda Lyon

Based on the ballet *Petrushka*, with music by
Igor Stravinsky

NELSON
YOUNG WORLD

It was the day of the Shrove
Tide Fair in old St. Petersburg.
Snow still lay upon the ground,
but the golden domes of the
churches and palaces all
sparkled in the sun.

6

The streets were full of people.
Everybody was going to the
Admiralty Square, where the
Fair was being held.

7

In the Admiralty Square, merchants
from all over Russia had set up
their stalls. Some were selling
furs from the great forests of the north.

Others were selling
beautiful silks, rare spices
and perfumes from the distant
lands of Asia.

There were jugglers, acrobats,
sword swallowers and fire eaters
to entertain the crowds. There
was a fortune teller, and an old

10

organ grinder and his dancing
companion. Everything was
colour, noise, excitement.

11

In the middle of the Admiralty
Square was a small travelling
theatre. The curtains were
drawn across the stage.

Then a showman stepped out
between the curtains. He started
to play a tune on his flute.
People stopped to listen, and
a crowd gathered round the stage.

The showman put his flute
under his arm, clapped his
hands, and pulled back the
curtains.

Up on the stage
stood three puppets: a Moor,
a Ballerina, and a sad looking
clown called Petrushka.

15

"Ladies and Gentlemen," the
showman announced. "I present
to you the finest puppets in
the world. I made them. I can
make them come alive. Just watch."

The showman touched each puppet
with his flute. As he did so,
each seemed to jerk into life.

17

Then, at a signal from the
showman, the puppets started
to dance to a lively Russian
folk tune.

It was a favourite with the
crowd. They clapped and
laughed and threw money on to
the stage.

At the end of the dance, the
showman closed the curtains
again and collected the money.
20 The crowd went away.

But behind the curtain, the
three puppets continued to
live in a strange, sad little
world of their own.

Petrushka loved the Ballerina.
But because he was only made
of cloth and straw, he could
never tell her so. He sat in
his tiny room up on the stage,
and hung his head sadly.

To Petrushka's surprise and
delight, the Ballerina came
tripping into his room. He
wanted to say: "Hallo, my
pretty little Ballerina. You
have made me feel so happy by
coming to see me." He got up
and started to dance with her.

But she soon grew tired of
him, and left the room again.
Petrushka banged his fists
against the wall in his despair.

In his room, the Moor was
playing with a coconut. He
was trying to open it. He
tried to break it open with
his sabre. He picked it up
and dropped it on the floor.
Finally, he kicked it round
the room in a fit of bad
temper.

The Ballerina came to see
him. She started to dance
a graceful little waltz.

The Moor tried to join in,
but he was much too clumsy
for her dainty steps.

Petrushka had been watching
through a crack in the wall.

"That clumsy, bad tempered Moor
has no right to dance with my
Ballerina," he thought. He
felt so jealous that he rushed
into the room.

Petrushka tried to beat the
Moor with his fists. "Perhaps
the Ballerina will love me for
being so brave," he thought.

But the Moor picked up his
sabre and chased poor Petrushka
from the room.

Outside, in the Admiralty
Square, the Fair was as gay
and noisy as ever. People
stepped aside as a man led
a big black bear on a chain.

Other people were joining
hands and dancing, round
and round the great open square.

Suddenly, from the back of the little theatre rushed Petrushka. Close behind him came the Moor, still waving his sabre.

"Look at those puppets," someone cried. "They really have come alive."

People stopped and stared. They could hardly believe their eyes.

TEAT

37

They watched as the Moor
caught up with Petrushka.
They saw the Moor strike
Petrushka with his sabre.

They saw Petrushka fall to
the ground, and then lie
still, just as if he had
been killed.

The old showman came out and
picked Petrushka up.

"Don't worry, folks," he
laughed. "See, it's only a
40 puppet after all."

The showman shook Petrushka
until the sawdust ran out of
his arm. Then he threw him
behind the curtain.

But that night, as the showman was coming back across the empty square, he suddenly stopped.

There was a strange little figure
dancing about in the moonlight.
Who could it be?

It was Petrushka's ghost. It
appeared above the theatre.
It waved its fists and made
faces at the showman.

"You made me come alive,
and gave me feelings I couldn't
understand," it seemed to be
saying. "You laughed at my
poor broken body in front of
all the people. Now I shall
haunt you for the rest of
your life."

45